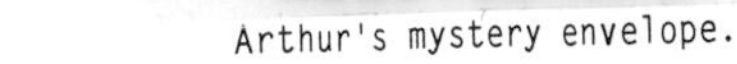

CHICAGO PUBLIC LIBRARY
WHITNEY YOUNG BRANCH
7901 S KING DR. 60619

Arthur's Mystery Envelope

A Marc Brown ARTHUR Chapter Book

Arthur's Mystery Envelope

Little, Brown and Company
Boston New York Toronto London

First Edition

Text by Stephen Krensky, based on the teleplay by Sheilarae Carpentier Lau

Text has been reviewed and assigned a reading level by Laurel S. Ernst, M.A., Teachers College, Columbia University, New York, New York; reading specialist, Chappaqua, New York

ISBN 0-316-11546-0 (hc)
ISBN 0-316-11547-9 (pb)
Library of Congress Catalog Card Number 97-074756

10 9 8 7 6 5 4 3 2 1

WOR (hc)
COM-MO (pb)

Published simultaneously in Canada by Little, Brown & Company (Canada) Limited

Printed in the United States of America

For my wonderful editor, Maria Modugno,
who really knows how to polish Arthur's star

Chapter 1

The cafeteria at Lakewood Elementary was filled with kids eating lunch. Some of them had brought sandwiches from home. The rest were eating school lunches. Today's choices featured a mystery meat covered in gravy.

A few teachers wandered between the tables trying to keep the noise under control.

"Let's keep it down," said Mr. Ratburn. He shook his head. "I don't think anyone's listening."

Miss Sweetwater nodded. "Or maybe they just can't hear us," she said.

At one of the middle tables, Arthur and his friends were finishing up.

Arthur was poking at his food with a fork. "Even without the gravy," he said, "we'd have no idea where this came from."

"Ready for action, boys?" Francine asked.

"Ready," said Arthur. He put aside his tray.

"And waiting," said Buster.

They started a game of milk hockey. Francine and Sue Ellen made up one team. Arthur and Buster were the other. They used a crushed milk carton as a puck, hitting it back and forth the length of the table.

Francine dodged left and flipped the carton past Arthur's hand. Buster tried to stop it, but the puck slid past him off the table.

"Goal!" said Muffy. She was the official scorekeeper.

Francine smiled. "That didn't take long," she said.

Arthur flexed his hands. "We just take a little while to warm up."

"All right," said Sue Ellen. "Let us know when you're nice and toasty."

"Maybe we'll need a substitution," said Buster. He turned to Binky Barnes. "Do you want a turn?"

"No," said Binky, crushing another carton with his fist. He just liked making pucks.

"Attention, please!"

Miss Tingley, the school secretary, was speaking over the loudspeaker.

"Arthur Read, please report to Principal Haney's office immediately."

A hush fell over the room. Everyone was staring at Arthur. Buster's mouth was wide open. Binky's hand had frozen in mid-crush.

"Uh-oh!" said Francine.

"I'll say," said Muffy.

Sue Ellen just shook her head.

"You're in real trouble now, Arthur," said Buster. Sometimes Mr. Haney yelled at him for running through the halls. But he had been to the *office* only once — for putting sneezing powder on Mr. Ratburn's desk.

"Are you all right, Arthur?" Francine asked.

"I-I guess."

"He doesn't look all right," said Sue Ellen. "He looks like one of those deer you read about. The ones who stare into the car headlights."

"He's in shock," said Binky. "He's not used to visiting the principal's office. I could get there blindfolded with one hand tied behind my back."

"What did you do, Arthur?" asked Francine.

Arthur shook his head. "I don't know. Nothing that I can think of."

Binky snorted. "Don't bother trying that excuse on Mr. Haney. It never works for me."

Arthur stood up. "Well, I guess I should go."

"Nice knowing you, Arthur," said Francine.

"Good luck," said Buster. "And if you're not planning to finish those potatoes . . ." He pointed to Arthur's plate.

Arthur slid over his tray. "Help yourself," he said. "I just lost my appetite."

Chapter 2

When Arthur got back to the classroom, his friends rushed to his side.

"You survived!" said Buster.

"With no obvious signs of torture," Binky added. He looked a little disappointed.

"What happened?" asked Francine.

Arthur let out a sigh. "Mr. Haney gave me this." He held up a large brown envelope. "He said it was for my mom."

"That's it?" asked Muffy. She reached out for a closer look. "What does it say? Is it sealed?"

Francine grabbed the envelope. "It's sealed, all right." She held it up to the light. "And too thick to read through."

"Give it a shake," said Buster, cocking his ears.

Francine shook the envelope for a moment. It rustled softly. "That doesn't tell us much," she said.

Binky folded his arms. "Let's just open it."

"I can't," said Arthur. "It's addressed to my mother. And look what's stamped on it: PRIVATE and CONFIDENTIAL."

"That's a bad sign," said Buster. "Good news is never private."

"Besides," said Binky, "you can't start making excuses until you know what kind of trouble you're in."

"Didn't Mr. Haney give you any clues at all?" Francine asked.

"He said it was important," said Arthur,

taking back the envelope. "That was about it."

"If it was good news," said Muffy, "Mr. Haney would have told you. My mother always tells me right away if we've gotten a new limousine or if the cook is making a special dessert for dinner."

"He didn't say anything like that," Arthur admitted.

"That means it's bad news," said Francine. "The question is, how bad is it?"

This was not a question Arthur wanted to think about.

Binky laughed. "Oooooh! I'll bet you lost a library book."

"I don't think Mr. Haney gets involved with overdue library books," said Arthur. "Besides, I just returned all mine."

"Oh, no!" said Francine.

"What?" said Muffy.

"Tell us," said Buster.

"Tell me!" said Arthur.

"Never mind," said Francine. "It's too terrible to think about."

Arthur turned pale. "That's why you have to tell me."

"All right," said Francine. "But you forced me into it." She shuddered. "What if you didn't pass Mr. Ratburn's history test?"

Arthur frowned. The big test had been the week before. It had been a hard one.

"Remember, Arthur? You told me afterward that you wrote how the Pilgrims came to America in 1620."

"Francine, the Pilgrims *did* come to America in 1620."

She looked surprised. "Really?"

Everyone else nodded.

"Well, still . . ." Francine tapped the envelope. "The proof is right here. And if you failed that test, you might fail the whole year. You know what that means: summer school."

Arthur sat down in his chair and thought about his fate. Summer school. Perhaps the two most dreaded words in the English language.

He saw himself chained to the wall of a dark dungeon. Outside the barred window, he could hear his friends playing. He looked out through the bars. Buster and the Brain were setting up a tent for camping. Muffy and Prunella were Rollerblading.

Arthur looked around his cell. He was alone — with only some thick, dusty books for company. Then the guard, Mr. Ratburn, walked in. He was slurping ice cream from a cone. A few drops fell on the stones, just beyond Arthur's reach.

"Snap out of it, Arthur!" said Buster.

Arthur looked at his friend blankly.

"You know what they say," Buster went

PRIVATE

on. "Those who don't learn their history are doomed to repeat it."

Arthur sighed. History or not, he felt doomed for sure.

Chapter 3

Arthur could have taken the envelope straight home after school. But he didn't.

"Mr. Haney didn't say anything about *when* you should deliver the envelope," the Brain had told him. "Under international law, you have the right to make a plan."

They were sitting in a booth at the Sugar Bowl. Buster and Francine were there, too. Prunella and Muffy were seated behind them.

Arthur had bought some candy, but he wasn't eating it. He was just moving it around in front of him. The candy was shaped in a rectangle with a big question mark inside it.

The Brain was staring hard at Arthur's envelope. "If only I could use X-ray vision . . . ," he said.

Buster grabbed the envelope from him. "We have to take action! I don't want to spend all summer doing fun stuff without you." He pushed the envelope toward the edge of the table. "Hey, what if you accidentally lost it?"

He shoved the envelope onto the floor. "It could end up in the trash. Or a shredder. Then bulldozed into a landfill. Only the seagulls would read it there. And we don't have to worry what they think."

"That's true," said Arthur.

Prunella picked up the envelope.

"Don't listen to him, Arthur. He doesn't look ahead. You need to think of something that won't be blamed on you in the end." She paused. "Maybe you could hide it in the laundry basket — and it could get *washed.*" She picked up the envelope and held it carefully as if it were wet and dripping. "She won't be able to read it, but you won't be blamed."

"Laundry," said Arthur. "Interesting."

"Not interesting," said Muffy. "Risky. You need to get it as far away from your house as possible. Buy it a first-class ticket to Alaska or Timbuktu."

"I don't have that kind of money," said Arthur.

He looked at the clock. It was time to go home.

Everyone went outside.

Francine was still frowning. "There must be some way out of this," she said.

The Brain looked down at the storm drain. "You could drop it in here," he said. "The current would carry it into Bear Lake and from there to the Otter River. Once it

THE SUGAR BOWL
PRIVATE

was in the harbor, it would be carried out to sea — maybe even to Europe. When it eventually washed up on shore, it's possible a mother might find it. But she probably wouldn't understand English, so you'd be safe."

"Europe is far away," said Arthur.

Francine plucked the envelope from the Brain's hand. "Don't do it, Arthur," she said. "If you try to lose it, you'll be in double trouble — for losing it *and* for whatever you did in the first place."

She handed the envelope back to him.

"The whole thing doesn't seem fair," said Arthur. "I didn't do anything! I'll just have to give the envelope to my mother and see what happens."

He had hoped saying that would make him feel better. It didn't.

"That's a last resort," said the Brain. "But, of course, the choice is yours."

Chapter 4

"Hello!" Arthur called out softly.

No one was in the kitchen except his dog, Pal. Arthur knew his mother was home, though. Her car was in the driveway.

"But she could be busy," he told Pal. "In fact, I'm sure of it. She could be working or helping D.W. or taking care of baby Kate. I don't want to disturb her."

Pal barked.

"Are you hungry?" said Arthur.

Pal wagged his tail.

Arthur put down his backpack on the counter. One corner of Mr. Haney's envelope was sticking out of the flap. Then he began rinsing out Pal's food dish.

"Mr. Haney told me the envelope was for Mom," Arthur explained to Pal. "But he didn't say what was in it."

Pal barked.

"No," said Arthur, "I can't eat the envelope."

Pal barked again.

"No, I can't bury it in the backyard, either."

He put the empty dish on the floor. Pal whined with disappointment.

"All my friends think the news must be bad," Arthur went on.

Pal contined to whine.

"Francine thinks I failed Mr. Ratburn's history test. She says I'll have to go to summer school." Arthur made a face.

Pal jumped up and down at his side.

Arthur fetched the dog food from the pantry. "Maybe I'll just leave it out and not say anything. Mr. Haney said I should bring it home to her. He didn't say I actually had to *give* it to her. Maybe she won't even notice it."

Arthur lay the dish on the table, then opened his backpack. He removed the envelope carefully and put it on the table.

"What's that?"

Arthur whirled to find his sister D.W. standing in the doorway.

"What's what?"

D.W. pointed. "The envelope, silly."

"Nothing!" he shouted. He leaned on the table. "It's just a dumb old envelope. People could walk by this envelope for weeks and not even notice it. And even if they did notice it, they wouldn't bother to open a boring envelope like this."

"That's a lot of nothing," said D.W. "You sure are acting weird."

"I'm not acting weird," said Arthur. He straightened up and folded his arms. "I'm worried. I mean, I'm not worried. I'm hurried. That's it. Hurried. Third grade is very busy."

D.W. climbed onto a chair and stared into Arthur's eyes. "You don't fool me," she said. "I know *worry* when I see it."

Arthur blinked. "You do?"

D.W. nodded. "Yup. You get wrinkles."

"I do?"

She nodded. "I'm not surprised. You could worry about lots of things. Like maybe someday you'll be too old for birthday presents. Or maybe you think there really is a boogeyman, and he's just waiting for the first night you forget to check under your bed."

Arthur sighed. "Those are regular worries. Everyday worries. I can handle those."

D.W. gave him a careful look. "You mean there's *more?* Come on, spill the beans."

CONFIDENTIAL
PRIVATE

"All right, all right!" said Arthur. "The principal just gave me this envelope for Mom. That's all. Now leave me alone!"

But D.W. wasn't finished yet. She took a look at the envelope. "What are these words?" she asked.

"Which words?"

"These big words on the front."

"PRIVATE and CONFIDENTIAL."

D.W. frowned. "I know PRIVATE. What does CON-FI-DEN-TEE-UL mean?"

Arthur sighed. "That only Mom can look at it."

D.W.'s eyes opened wide. She got down from the chair and skipped toward the hall, singing,

"Arthur's in trouble,
Arthur's in trouble."

For once Arthur didn't argue with her. He knew she was right.

Chapter 5

The good news was that D.W. suddenly stopped singing. The bad news was that she stopped because she had bumped into her mother.

"Slow down, sweetie. We can't afford to put a traffic light in here."

Mrs. Read gave D.W. a quick kiss. Her hands were full of papers.

"What a day! If I had two heads and four hands, I'd still be behind."

Mrs. Read was an accountant. She always got a little frazzled at tax time.

"Mom, Arthur's acting a little weird. He brought home a —"

"Hey!" said Arthur. "That's none of your —"

"Hush, Arthur!" said his mother. "Not now, D.W. I've got a few calls to make."

She put her papers down on the counter.

"Arthur, what is this?"

Arthur cringed. "That?"

"Yes, that." She pointed to the envelope and Pal's dish beside it. "On the table."

"The table? Here? In the kitchen?"

His mother folded her arms. "Yes, the kitchen table. Since when does Pal eat there?"

Arthur let out a deep breath.

"He doesn't."

"Then why did you leave his dish on the table?" She put it down on the floor. "Honestly, Arthur, I expect you to be more careful."

While Arthur fidgeted, Mrs. Read picked up the phone and dialed a number. She left a message with the secretary.

PAL
PRIVATE
CONFIDENTIAL

“That’s my third try this afternoon. That man is just impossible to reach.” She glanced at Arthur. “Is everything all right? You look a little pale.”

“Of course,” said Arthur. “I was just thinking about, um . . . setting the table for dinner.” He pulled out some forks and knives from a drawer and began placing them in front of each chair.

“Mail call!” said Mr. Read, arriving with a bundle of letters. He dropped them on top of Arthur’s envelope.

“How is everyone today?”

“Dear, you have whipped cream behind your ear.”

“Really? I thought I had cleaned it all up.” He scraped the cream off with his finger. “I was experimenting with a new dessert.”

Mr. Read was very busy with his catering business.

"I hope no one was hurt," said Mrs. Read.

Mr. Read sighed. "Only the piecrust didn't survive."

The phone rang.

"I'll get it," said Mrs. Read. She picked up the mail and the envelope as she answered the phone. "Hello? Oh, hi, Leah."

She started to look through the mail.

One letter went into the wastebasket.

"No, no, I'm not disappointed you called. I was just expecting to hear from Herb."

She put a bill aside for later.

"I needed some paperwork from him."

She flipped through a magazine.

"Yes, I know. It's all due Monday."

Arthur watched his mother with an increasing sense of doom. He edged his way to the door. His mother had reached Mr. Haney's envelope.

Suddenly the water on the stove began bubbling over.

"Oh, I've got to run," said Mrs. Read. "Talk to you later, Leah." She hung up the phone and dropped the envelope on the edge of the counter. She turned back to the stove.

The envelope teetered for a moment — and then fell into the wastebasket.

Arthur slumped with relief. He was innocent. He hadn't put the envelope in the trash. Some other hand had guided it there. It was fate. It was destiny. It was meant to be.

Chapter 6

Dinner was hard to swallow. How could Arthur concentrate on eating? Every time he looked up, he saw the envelope peeking at him from the wastebasket.

Even the fact that they were having hamburgers and potato puffs hadn't cheered him up. His partly eaten hamburger sat on the edge of his plate like a crescent moon. Usually he piled the potato puffs into a castle wall and then lined up the green beans like alligators in the moat. But tonight he had only stamped the puffs and beans down with his fork. They looked like little shredded carpets.

"Are you trying to save wear and tear on your teeth, Arthur?" asked his mother.

Arthur looked confused.

She pointed to his plate. "All that mashing. You still have to eat them, you know. We don't want to waste food."

Arthur took a small bite.

His father helped himself to some salad. "You're awfully quiet tonight, Arthur," he said.

Arthur squirmed in his chair. "We worked hard in school today." He looked at his father. "When you were in school, were tests important?"

"Oh, yes. We didn't have all the different projects you kids have today. Sometimes a single test could be half our whole grade."

"That much?"

His father smiled. "Definitely. I wouldn't

say you kids have it easy, but you do have more choices."

"Most important," said Mrs. Read, "we want you to do your best."

"I always do my best," said D.W., who was swapping potato puffs with Kate. "It's all part of my plan."

"What plan is that, sweetie?" asked her mother.

"Her plan for world domination," said Arthur.

"Arrrthur!" said his father.

"Sorry." Arthur changed the subject. "Do you think every part of school is important? I mean, don't some parts matter more than others?"

Mr. Read shook his head. "That's hard to say. At your age I never planned on having a catering business. And even though my business is food, I still need to know math for planning and how to write for advertising."

"What about, um, history?" said Arthur. "That wouldn't matter so much, would it?"

"History's important, too," said his father. "I might want to study old recipes or create a meal with some historical theme."

"I see," said Arthur, wishing he didn't.

"It makes sense to learn about everything," said his mother. "You can't tell when it might come in handy later on." She looked down the table. "Arthur, pass me the potato puffs, please."

Arthur picked up the bowl.

D.W. smiled. "Arthur, isn't there anything else you'd like to give Mom while you're at it?"

Arthur just barely kept himself from kicking D.W. under the table. "Just my thanks," he said, "for making this great dinner."

He forked up some mashed puffs and beans and filled his mouth.

His mother looked at him. "Thank you, Arthur — I think."

She might have said more, but the phone rang. She jumped up to get it.

Saved by the bell, thought Arthur — at least for now.

Chapter 7

After dinner, Arthur went to his room to do his homework.

Think of a word that rhymes with rope *and* hope.

"Arrghhh!" said Arthur.

He switched quickly to math. The first problem involved cutting a rectangle in half.

"I wish I could cut that envelope in half," said Arthur.

Another question was about a mailbag filled with letters. There was no mention of the *E* word, but that was all Arthur could think about.

He began doodling on the edge of his paper. He started with a big rectangle, an enormous rectangle, the largest rectangle in the world.

But was it only a rectangle? No, it was a giant envelope, and it was chasing Arthur down a hill. It tumbled end over end. Arthur could barely keep ahead of it.

"Don't run," the envelope was saying. "I know you'll fit nicely inside me. And don't worry. I will never let you out."

"No, thank you," said Arthur. "I'll get flattened." He ran faster.

"That's not my fault," said the envelope, huffing and puffing. "I'm just not in very good shape."

Arthur rubbed his eyes. He needed a break.

He took a peek in Kate's room. She was already asleep.

"Babies are lucky," he muttered. "They

don't have to worry about envelopes. Or history tests. Or summer school. They only have to look cute and fill their diapers."

Kate turned in her sleep, and her blanket slipped off her.

Arthur put it back. "The good old days," he sighed.

His mother was sitting in her office. She was chewing on a pencil and humming while she worked. Arthur tiptoed past the door. He found his father and D.W. watching *The Karaoke Kittens* show on TV.

The kittens were wearing straw hats and dancing in a line while they sang.

"Those kittens are crazy," said D.W. "Watch carefully now. This is the best part."

"How do you know?" asked her father.

Arthur sat down. "She's seen this episode eighty-four times," he explained.

"And it just gets better and better," said D.W. She shook her head in time with the music.

Her father hummed along. "Not every kitten can dance like that," he pointed out. "It takes a lot of practice."

A commercial came on.

"Is the stress of everyday life getting you down?"

Arthur nodded.

"Do you feel like you're no longer in control?"

Arthur nodded again.

"The pounding, the pounding. It just won't stop."

Arthur cradled his head in his arms.

"For the chance to feel like your old self again, try Painfree or Painfree Plus. Headache relief is just minutes away."

Arthur stood up. If only he could take a pill to get rid of his problem. But things were not that easy.

"You really look tired, Arthur," said his father.

"I am," Arthur admitted.

"Sshhhh!" said D.W. "The kittens are going to sing 'Fur Ball.' I love that song."

Arthur didn't stay to hear it. With a quiet "Good night," he went up to bed.

Chapter 8

As Arthur got ready for bed, he found himself looking at his pillow. He had never noticed before how much it looked like a stuffed envelope.

While brushing his teeth, Arthur brought his face right up to the mirror. His teeth lined up in little square rows.

Almost like envelopes, he thought.

Everywhere he looked — the wallpaper, the carpeting, the pattern on his blanket — he saw envelopes. They came in every shape and size.

"I have envelopes on the brain," he

decided. "What I need is a good night's sleep."

Arthur climbed into bed and pulled up the covers.

"Are you still awake, Arthur?"

D.W. was standing in the doorway.

"No. I'm sound asleep. You're a bad dream. Go away."

"If you're sound asleep, how can you tell me to go away?"

Arthur sat up. "What do you want?"

"I want to know about the trouble you're in."

"There's no trouble, D.W."

She was not convinced. "What was in that mysterious envelope?"

"I don't know," Arthur said honestly.

"Mom didn't mention it to you?"

"No, she didn't."

"Oh." D.W. was disappointed. "Don't worry. I'm sure you'll get in trouble for something else."

"Thanks, D.W. That makes me feel much better."

"Anytime," said D.W., and went back to her room.

Arthur stared at the ceiling. Strictly speaking, he had told D.W. the truth. His mother *hadn't* mentioned to him what was inside the envelope. Of course, that was only because she hadn't *seen* it yet. The envelope was still sitting in the wastebasket.

Why can't it just stay there? thought Arthur.

He closed his eyes for what seemed like only a second.

His eyes opened.

Arthur heard some paper rustling. What was making that sound? He got out of bed and listened.

The sound was coming from downstairs.

Arthur followed the noise into the kitchen. The wastebasket was shaking — as if something was bouncing around inside it. Arthur looked down. Mr. Haney's envelope was growing bigger right before his eyes! The wastebasket could no longer hold it.

Arthur pulled the envelope free and ran upstairs. The envelope was flapping in his arms. It was getting too big to carry. Arthur dragged it along the floor to the bathroom. He hoisted it into the tub and drew the shower curtain.

The curtain shook and trembled.

Arthur screamed — and fled downstairs into his mother's arms.

"What's going on?" she asked.

Arthur grabbed her arm and pulled.

"We have to get out of the house, Mom. It's getting too big!"

As they stepped outside, one corner of the envelope wriggled through a window. Another popped out of the chimney.

"What's going on?" asked his mother.

"It's the envelope," yelled Arthur. "Don't open it! It could be something horrible!"

PRIVATE
CONFIDEN

At that moment the roof flew off the house. The top of the envelope rose up, and the flap opened.

D.W. popped out.

"You tricked me, Arthur," she said. "You haven't even told Mom yet."

"Noooooo!" cried Arthur.

Chapter 9

Arthur woke up. His hands were crossed in front of his face.

"I can't go on this way," he muttered. "Even summer school would be better than this."

He walked downstairs. His father was still watching TV. It was some kind of cooking show.

"Parsley, sage, rosemary, and thyme may make for a good song title, but don't use them together as seasonings."

"It might be worth trying," Mr. Read said to himself. "Maybe in a soup . . ."

Arthur kept going. His feet felt like lead,

and his legs seemed to be moving in slow motion.

The envelope was still in the wastebasket. Arthur picked it out.

He walked over to the dining room, where his mother had her work area.

The light was still on.

Arthur took a deep breath. "It's going to keep bothering me until I get this over with."

He entered the dining room.

"Do you have a second, Mom?"

His mother put down her pen. "For you, two seconds. But why are you up so late?"

Arthur took a deep breath. "That's what I need to talk to you about. I was supposed to do something right away when I got home. But I was worried I might be in trouble, so I didn't do it, and now I'm afraid you're going to get mad —"

"Slow down, Arthur! What's going on? You can tell me. I won't get mad."

TAX.

"Promise?"

She nodded.

Arthur handed her the envelope. She slit it open and glanced inside.

"Ah! Here it is!" She frowned. "Arthur, I've been waiting for this all night."

Arthur looked down at the floor. "You said you wouldn't get mad."

"Yes, yes, I did." His mother took a deep breath. "Well, I'm not mad exactly. *Frustrated* would be a better word. I'm very frustrated. I've been trying to reach Herb for hours. I need this information."

"But this is from Mr. Haney."

"Herb is his first name."

She glanced through the papers.

"Um, Mom?"

"Hmmmm. . . . Yes, Arthur?"

"What's in there?"

His mother looked up. "Tax documents. I'm doing his tax return."

"Nothing to do with me?"

"Not unless you want to help Mr. Haney pay his taxes!"

Arthur laughed. "Good-bye, summer school," he murmured.

Mrs. Read put down her papers for a moment. "Now I think I understand," she said. "But Arthur, even if this was about you, we would need to know."

"What if it was something bad?"

His mother sighed. "Putting off bad news doesn't make it get any better. And sometimes it makes it worse. Besides, Dad and I can't help you with a problem if we don't know you have one."

Arthur nodded. "I guess that's true."

"Well, we can talk more in the morning. Now back to bed, honey. It's late."

She gave him a kiss.

All that worrying for nothing, thought Arthur. He had tortured himself all afternoon and evening for no good reason.

"Cheer up, Arthur," said his mother.

"You're not disappointed, I hope. Because if you really want to be in trouble, I'm sure I could arrange —"

"Good night, Mom!" Arthur said hurriedly, and bolted for the door.

Chapter 10

It was too late for Arthur to call his friends, but he could imagine their reactions.

"You're still alive?" Francine would say. "Way to go!"

Buster would be pleased, too. "Now we'll be together all summer! If you get in any trouble then, I'll be right there beside you."

"Rats," Binky would say. "You got off the hook again? I can't believe it."

As Arthur was about to head up the stairs, he saw D.W. waiting for him.

"So, tell me what happened!" she said.

"Are you grounded for a year? Off to jail? Can I have your room?"

"Back to bed, you two!" their mother called out.

"I'm just getting a drink," said D.W. She stared at Arthur. "I'm waiting. . . ."

Arthur shrugged. "Sorry to disappoint you, D.W., but there's nothing to tell. I don't know where you get these crazy ideas."

"Crazy ideas? Where do I get them?" She stopped to think. "Let me see. I wasn't the one frozen in terror. Or jumpy as a frog."

"Frozen? Jumpy?" Arthur's eyes opened wide. "What an imagination!"

"Come on," said D.W. "Tell me. Are you moving into the garage? Is Pal moving there with you? Are we —"

"Enough questions," said Arthur. "I'm not telling you anything."

"You're not?"

Arthur smiled. "D.W., this is one mystery you'll have to solve on your own."

She made a face at him, but Arthur didn't care. He felt better at last.